W9-AVA-729

Loop the Loop

By
BARBARA DUGAN
Pictures by
JAMES STEVENSON

Greenwillow Books
New York

Watercolor paints and a black pen
were used for the full-color art.
The text type is ITC Galliard.

Printed in Hong Kong by South China
Printing Company (1988) Ltd.

First Edition 10 9 8 7 6 5 4 3 2 1

Library of Congress
Cataloging-in-Publication Data

Dugan, Barbara.
Loop the loop / by Barbara Dugan;
pictures by James Stevenson.
p. cm.
Summary: A young girl and an old woman
form a friendship that lasts even after
the woman enters a nursing home.
ISBN 0-688-09647-6.
ISBN 0-688-09648-4 (lib. bdg.)
[1. Old age—Fiction. 2. Friendship—Fiction.]
I. Stevenson, James (date). II. Title.
PZ7.D87817Lo 1992
[E]—dc20 90-21727 CIP AC

FOR MICHAEL,
LUKE, AND
JOHN PATRICK

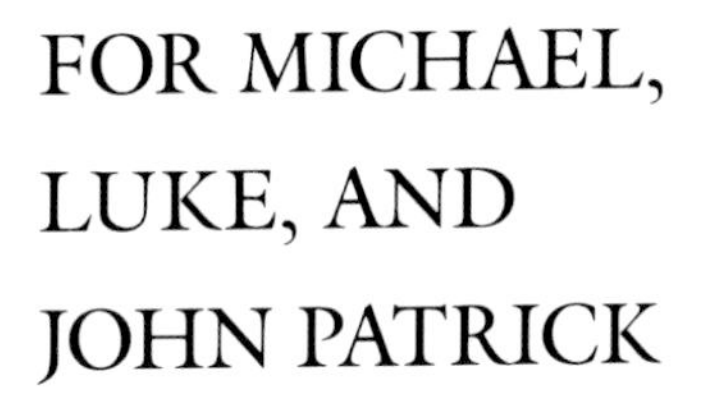

Anne was in her front yard giving instructions to her doll. "Eleanor," she said, "you must keep warm," and she folded the blanket in, over, and up around her baby doll's chin. "Eat," she said, pressing the tip of the baby bottle to the hole between Eleanor's lips. "And don't spit up."

"That's good advice," called a voice from the sidewalk. Anne looked up to find the voice and saw a familiar face. It was the old woman in the wheelchair. Anne had never spoken to the woman, but often she watched her as she wheeled by on warm days, pushed by the young lady with the high ponytail and the white shoes.

"I don't believe we've been introduced," said the old woman.

The young lady, the helper, smiled and nodded her head, and Anne quietly told the old woman her name.

"Anne Boleyn, Anne Frank, Anna Karenina," said the old woman. "I *like* it, Anne. My name is Methuselah."

"Mrs. Simpson," said the young lady, "that's not your name."

"Well, that's who I feel like. I'm Methuselah, and I'm nine hundred and sixty-nine years old. Who are you?"

Anne shrugged. "Nobody."

"Nobody!" Mrs. Simpson shouted. "That's good. Maybe I'll feel like nobody tomorrow. Forward, Bonnie. Good-bye, Nobody."

Anne watched them wheel away. Mrs. Simpson had pulled a hand out from under her lap blanket, and there, tethered to the end of her long white finger, was a yo-yo. Arcing her wrist and releasing it—down and back, down and back—Mrs. Simpson spun and reeled the wooden spool.

The next morning out under the oak tree Anne set up a lemonade stand: a card table, a cigar-box cash register, sunbonnets for her and Eleanor, and a frosted pitcher of pink lemonade. REFRESHMINTS, Anne wrote across an empty washing machine box, and posted the price of lemonade.
She set the box near the sidewalk and sat down to watch her neighborhood go through the motions of the morning.

The Pelmar twins strutted by on their way to the summer-school bus, talking about everything except lemonade.

The garbage collector said, “Oh, a lemonade stand,” but he kept his hands out of his pockets and on the trash cans.

The paperboy, late on his morning rounds, barely slowed his bike, lobbing the morning news over Anne’s head.

"Business will pick up this afternoon," Anne said to Eleanor. She opened the lid of the cigar box and counted nickels: two from Dad, three from Mom, one from the flap of her own loafer, and another from Eleanor. (Eleanor's lemonade had been paid for and gratefully drunk by Anne because sugar was no good for Eleanor.)

"Five more minutes, Anne," her mother called from the screen door. "You'll burn up in this heat."

Anne knew what had to be done. Across the cardboard she wrote SALE!, slashing her price, replacing it with TWO FOR ONE. Then, climbing on top of the box, she scouted the sidewalk for potential customers. The box caved in and Anne fell just as Bonnie and Mrs. Simpson rounded the corner.

"Mercy me," cried Mrs. Simpson. "Child, what are you doing on the ground?"

Anne rubbed grass off her knees and licked her fingers to get the dirt off. "Hello, Mrs. Simpson."

"Hello, hello. Who's the kid? I don't believe we've been introduced."

"Eleanor," Anne answered.

"*Eleanor Roosevelt*," Mrs. Simpson shouted. "What a woman! And what the doodad is this?"

"A lemonade stand," said Anne.

"*A lemonade stand*. I haven't seen one of those since the war. Did we win? Of course we did. How much?"

"Two glasses for a nickel," Anne said.

"Good heavens! The price hasn't changed. I'll take two. One at a time."

Anne carefully handed Mrs. Simpson a Dixie cup of lemonade. She gulped it down. Slammed the second one down, too. Then, turning to Bonnie, she asked if she might like some.

"No, thank you," said Bonnie.

"Tea at my house tomorrow, Anne," Mrs. Simpson announced. "Bring your lovely mother. You do have a mother?"

"Yes," said Anne.

"What's-her-face can come, too," said Mrs. Simpson, pointing a finger at Eleanor. "Two o'clock sharp. 'Camptown ladies sing this song, doodah, doodah. Camptown racetrack five miles long. Oh, doo-dah-day...'"

Anne and her mother arrived for tea in their pearls and party shoes. Eleanor was looking new; Anne had scrubbed her face and arms with cleanser.

"What do you want?" said Mrs. Simpson, greeting them at the front door.

Bonnie escorted them in, leading them through the kitchen littered with notes—"Turn off stove," "Take pills," "Unplug coffeepot"—and into the dining room.

"Where the devil is Bertrand?" said Mrs. Simpson, pulling her wheelchair up to the table. In a few moments there was the jingling of a tiny bell, and a gray cat jumped up on the stack of phone books piled on a chair. "Who told you you could come late? Put your napkin on. Fine. Be that way."

Bertrand lapped his saucer of milk. Anne, her mother, Mrs. Simpson, and Bonnie devoured chocolates, strawberries, macaroons, and mint tea.

Later, in front of the piano, Mrs. Simpson screamed, *"Take it from the top,"* and belted out "Hold That Tiger." She invited Anne to be the tiger and run around her living room. "Jump on the chairs if you like, dear," she said. "No one uses them, anyway."

Following that afternoon of tea, Anne met Bonnie and Mrs. Simpson every day of the days of June and July. In fine weather they explored the neighborhood and walked to the park. They threw bread to the ducks and pennies into the wishing well. On rainy days they played cards and Scrabble and dressed Bertrand up in Eleanor's clothes.

One day Mrs. Simpson took Anne aside and told her it was high time she learned something. "It's a crime," she said, "but"—she began to whisper—"very few children *really* know how to yo-yo." In a moment the yo-yo was launched—out of Mrs. Simpson's pocket, jetting down, crawling forward along the pavement.

"Walk the Dog," she hollered. With a snap of her wrist the yo-yo was in and out of her hand again, whirring circles in the air. "Ha-ha," she squealed. "Back off, Bonnie!"

"Mrs. Simpson," Bonnie said, "do you really think—"

"Around the World," yelled Mrs. Simpson. "Around the World." Still airborne, the yo-yo carved figure eights, bursting back and forth in front of the wheelchair, spinning loops. "What is it?"

"Loop the Loop," said Bonnie, "but I don't think—"

"Yes, Loop the Loop," said Mrs. Simpson. "Precisely. And now," she said, quieting the yo-yo, clutching it to her chest, "I need your help. Spit over your shoulder, Anne, dear. Can't do that? Never mind. I don't need the good luck." And she spun out the yo-yo, picking the string into a triangle, rocking the spool within it. "Get a load of this," she said, nodding to Eleanor. "Rock the Baby."

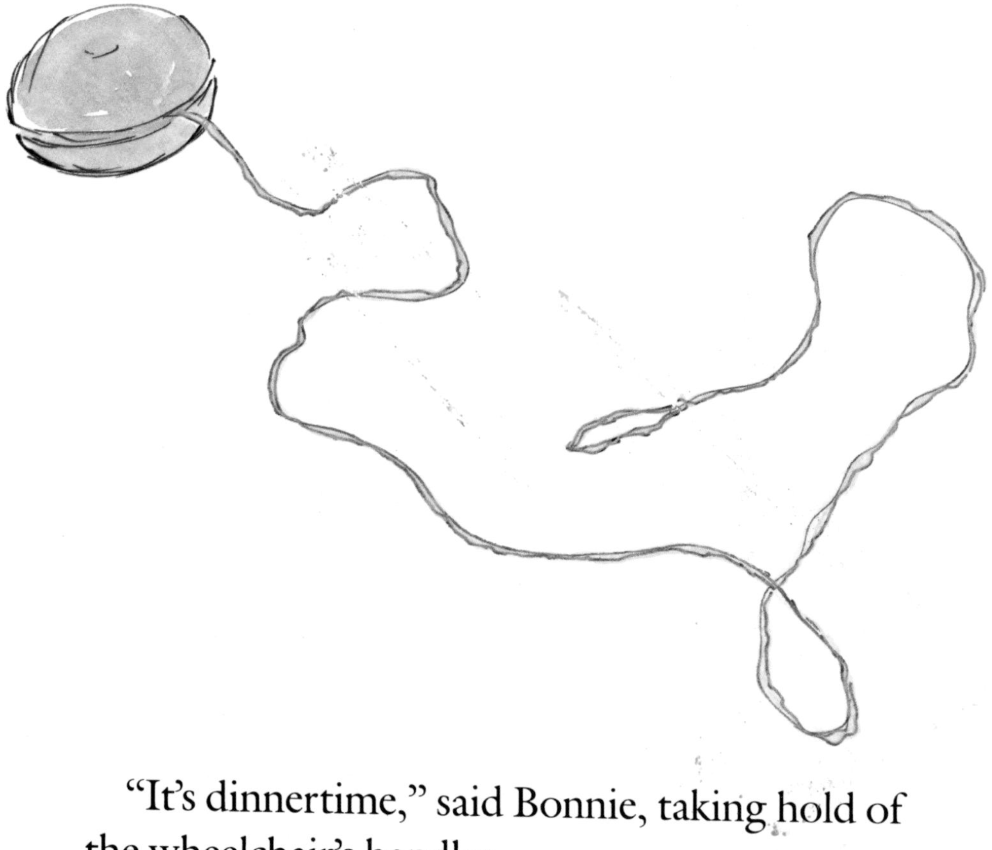

"It's dinnertime," said Bonnie, taking hold of the wheelchair's handles.

"I'm magnificent," said Mrs. Simpson, on the way home, "and I know it."

The next day Anne shook out her Snoopy bank and bought a yo-yo. At the library she checked out a book on yo-yo tricks. Anne didn't tell Mrs. Simpson what she had bought; she wanted to wait until she could perform some tricks of her own.

In August Mrs. Simpson broke her hip. "I can get out of this wheelchair by myself," she said before she fell.

In the hospital Mrs. Simpson lay on her side and faced the wall. "A kid!" she shouted when she saw Anne. "Hoorah, a kid. This place reeks of the dead and dying. Who are you? Well?"

"Anne. I'm Anne."

"I'm not buying those magazines, Anne."

"No, Mrs. Simpson," said Bonnie. "They're a gift."

"I don't know you," said Mrs. Simpson.

"It's me, Bonnie."

"'My bonnie lies over the ocean,'" said Mrs. Simpson. "'My bonnie lies over the sea. My bonnie lies over the ocean. Oh, bring back my bonnie to me.' Go home."

Bonnie took Anne's hand and put it inside Mrs. Simpson's. She set the vase of flowers on the table. Mrs. Simpson soon fell asleep.

"She doesn't know me," Anne said to Bonnie in the car.

"Maybe a part of her does," said Bonnie. "You were the best medicine she's ever had. I had hope this summer. But now with her broken hip, in the hospital...I don't know if she'll get well, Anne—if she'll be the same."

Anne cried, "I'm not going back to see her."

A week later Bonnie arrived at Anne's door with Bertrand in her arms. "Mrs. Simpson is being transferred to a nursing home," she said softly. "Bertrand can't live with her there. I know he'll be happy with you."

When Anne wasn't in school, she spent her time playing with Bertrand and practicing the yo-yo. She held many yo-yo contests in her room. Eleanor was the judge, and Anne always won.

It wasn't as easy with Bertrand. He refused to eat from his dish on the floor, and he kept escaping. Anne would find him at Mrs. Simpson's old house, scratching his back against the door, sleeping beneath the raspberry bushes.

"Bertrand is lonely for Mrs. Simpson," Anne said to her mother one day. "Eleanor might be lonesome for her, too."

"I wouldn't tell the nurse there's a cat in your backpack, Anne," said her mother on the way to the nursing home.

They found Mrs. Simpson in her room, Number 109.

"Hello," Anne called.

"You're too short to be my doctor," said Mrs. Simpson. "Also, there's a cat in your hair."

Bertrand squirmed out of the backpack, jumped off Anne's shoulder, leaped onto Mrs. Simpson's lap. He purred and nuzzled his face against her neck.

"Can I keep the kitty cat?" asked Mrs. Simpson.

Anne looked at her mother.

"I'm afraid he's just here for a visit," said her mother.

"I'm just here for a visit, too," said Mrs. Simpson. "I'm a vacationing ballerina. My shoes are in the closet."

"I'm a magician," said Anne. "I perform tricks." She plucked the yo-yo from her pocket, flung it down with a flick of her wrist. It halted an inch above the floor—suspended—still spinning. "The Sleeper," Anne announced.

"Bravo!" said Mrs. Simpson.

Figure eights burst back and forth. The yo-yo whirred, tracing circles in the air. "Loop the Loop," said Anne.

"Whoopee!" yelled Mrs. Simpson.

Just then the nurse walked in. She looked at the yo-yo, looked at Mrs. Simpson, looked at Bertrand, and she smiled. "I'm not reporting that I see a cat in here," she said, "because I know he's leaving shortly."

Anne scooped up Bertrand, eased him into the backpack, and fastened the string. "Two minutes and you're out, Bertrand, I promise." Then she took Eleanor and straightened her dress. She kissed her cheek and tucked her under Mrs. Simpson's arm.

"Don't worry," said Mrs. Simpson, "I know all about babies." She motioned to Anne with her finger.

Anne drew close.

"I was a baby once myself," Mrs. Simpson whispered. "I'll take good care of her until you come back. Where are you going?"

"Home," Anne said.

"Great place," said Mrs. Simpson.

Anne turned her face away and said good-bye. At the door she stopped and looked back. "You're magnificent, Mrs. Simpson."

"Oh, I know that," said Mrs. Simpson, and she held up Eleanor's arm and waved good-bye to Anne.